AND THE
ULTIMATE
RIDDLE

WRITTEN BY
MICHAEL ANTHONY STEELE

ILLUSTRATED BY
LEONEL CASTELLANI

BATMAN CREATED BY
BOB KANE WITH BILL FINGER

STONE ARCH BOOKS
a capstone imprint

Published by Stone Arch Books,
an Imprint of Capstone.
1710 Roe Crest Drive
North Mankato, Minnesota 56003
www.capstonepub.com

Library of Congress Cataloging-in-Publication Data is available
on the Library of Congress website.
ISBN: 978-1-4965-8721-3 (library binding)
ISBN: 978-1-4965-9199-9 (paperback)
ISBN: 978-1-4965-8725-1 (eBook PDF)

Summary: The Riddler is in a bit of a slump. It's bad enough
that Batman and his friends have foiled him again. But what's really
got him down is that he's no closer to learning the Caped Crusader's true
identity. Who is the man behind the mask? To find the answer, the Riddler
hatches a perilous plan that turns Batgirl and Robin into pawns. Can Batman
stop the Prince of Puzzles before he solves the ultimate riddle?

Designer: Kyle Grenz

Printed and bound in the USA.
PA100

TABLE OF CONTENTS

While still a boy, Bruce Wayne witnessed the death of his parents at the hands of a petty criminal. The tragic event changed the young billionaire's life forever. Bruce vowed to rid Gotham City of evil and keep its people safe from crime. After years of training his body and mind, he donned a new uniform and a new identity.

He became . . .

CHAPTER 1

MONKEY BUSINESS

KRASH!

A gloved hand smashed through a jewelry display case. Shards of broken glass glittered among the diamond necklaces and bracelets. The hand scooped up the jewelry and shoved a handful into a sack.

"Three minutes!" shouted a man in a lion mask. He checked his stopwatch as four other men and women in animal masks broke more display cases.

A man in a rhino mask laughed as he filled his sack with diamond rings. "No one can stop the Zoo Crew!"

"You said it," agreed a woman wearing a zebra mask.

A man in a monkey mask shook his head. "What a stupid name," he mumbled as he shoved necklaces into his bag.

"Come on!" Lion Mask shouted. "We now have two minutes and thirty seconds before the cops respond to the silent alarm."

"What about the Bat?" asked a woman in a tiger mask.

"My response time is much faster," answered a menacing voice from above.

The five criminals looked up to see a dark figure swoop in through the open skylight.

"It's . . . it's Batman!" shouted the man in the rhino mask.

With a blur of motion, four Batarangs whistled through the air. Each of the whirling bat-shaped weapons struck the criminals' wrists. They yelled in pain as they dropped their bags of loot.

"Let's get out of here," said the man in the lion mask.

The five thieves ran for the door as the Dark Knight swooped down from above. Batman tackled the man in the rhino mask and the woman in the zebra mask. They were knocked out before they hit the floor.

The remaining three crooks ran out of the store and onto the dark sidewalk. "Split up," ordered Lion Mask. "He can't catch us all."

"Wanna bet?" asked a young boy's voice. Robin somersaulted into view and landed in front of the crook with the lion mask.

The thief swung at the young crime fighter, but the Boy Wonder was too fast. He easily ducked the punch just before landing one of his own. The lion mask spun around the crook's head as he tumbled backward.

The woman in the tiger mask ran down the sidewalk. But she skidded to a stop when another crime fighter dropped down in front of her.

"Easy there, tiger," Batgirl said as she squared off against the thief.

The woman scratched at Batgirl as if she had real tiger claws. Batgirl blocked three attacks before delivering a spinning kick. The crook flew back to land on her unconscious boss.

"Leave the scratching to Catwoman," Batgirl said with a smirk.

Meanwhile, the man in the monkey mask huffed as he sprinted down the nearby alley. He glanced over his shoulder to make sure none of the crime fighters were following him. That's when he ran into a brick wall. Actually, it only *felt* like a brick wall. The man fell to the ground after smashing into Batman himself.

The stunned criminal raised his hands. "I surrender! I surrender!"

"Good," Batman said as he slapped handcuffs onto the thief's outstretched wrists.

The Dark Knight dragged the crook back up the alley. "That's the last of them," Batman said as he shoved Monkey Mask onto the pile of unconscious criminals.

Batgirl attached Monkey Mask's cuffs to the others. "This is certainly a colorful crew."

"Batman, look!" Robin pointed to the city skyline. A round spotlight reflected off the clouds above. There was a dark shape of a bat inside the spotlight—the Bat-Signal. It was how Police Commissioner Gordon called the Caped Crusader when there was trouble.

Batman put a hand to his ear to listen to a report on the police radio. "Solomon Grundy is smashing up the arts district."

"Want me to handle it?" asked Batgirl. She put her hands on her hips. "You two can take the rest of the night off," she joked.

"You know the rule," Batman said.

Batgirl sighed. "I know, I know. Small-time crooks are fine, but no taking on the heavy hitters by ourselves."

"And Solomon Grundy is a very heavy hitter," Robin said as he rubbed his jaw. "I know. I've been hit by him before."

Batman pressed a button on his Utility Belt. Within seconds, the Batmobile skidded to a stop on the street beside them. The hatch slid open.

"We'll take care of Grundy," Batman said as he and Robin leaped into the open car. "Wait here for the police to arrive and then catch up to us."

Batgirl gave the Dark Knight a casual salute. "You're the boss."

As the Batmobile sped away, Batgirl turned to the heap of criminals. "Since you're the only one still awake, maybe you can tell me something . . . What's with the animal masks?"

Unfortunately, the conscious criminal was gone. The monkey mask and a set of open handcuffs lay on the sidewalk beside the pile of crooks.

"Oh, boy," Batgirl said as she scanned the area. There was no sign of the missing thief. She turned to see if the crook was escaping down the street but was too late to see the metal sewer cover slide back into place.

* * *

Below the streets, the crook trudged through the filthy sewers. Without his monkey mask, the criminal was easy to recognize as one of Batman's biggest enemies—Edward Nygma, also known as the Riddler.

"I can't believe I had to team up with such a blundering bunch of dimwits," the Riddler grumbled as he stomped through the sludge.

The villain shook his head. "I used to be one of the great Gotham City villains. My name used to be feared right alongside the Joker or Two-Face. Now I'm stuck in the sewers like an animal . . . like Killer Croc!"

Nygma came to a metal ladder and began to climb. "If only I could solve the ultimate riddle . . . how to defeat Batman." The villain reached up and slowly opened the metal lid. He peeked around, but the street above was deserted.

"Good," he said as he carefully climbed out of the smelly sewer tunnel. "No sign of Batman or either of those Bat-brats."

As the Riddler dusted himself off, he remembered overhearing Batman's rule. "They're not allowed to face the heavy hitters alone, are they?" he asked. "So Batman worries about the youngsters, huh?"

A plan formed in Edward Nygma's mind. A plan that would take down Batman once and for all.

"Positively delightful," the Riddler said with a grin. Then his nose twitched and his smile faded. "But first . . . a shower."

CHAPTER 2

PUZZLE IN THE PARK

"Help!" a woman's voice shouted from a dark city park. "Help! Please!"

High above the city, Robin swung through the night. He released his line, did a flip, and landed on a nearby rooftop. As he leaned over the edge to get a better look, Batgirl landed silently behind him.

"You heard it too, huh?" Robin asked.

"Purse-snatching in the park," Batgirl said. "Lovely night for it."

Robin leaped off the edge of the roof. "Beat you there," he challenged as he spread his cape wide. The fabric filled with air and he glided toward the ground.

Meanwhile, Batgirl dove off the roof and kept her arms tight to her side. She zipped past Robin as she rocketed toward the ground. Then, at the last minute, she spread her cape and caught just enough air to direct herself toward a large tree.

Batgirl grabbed a thick branch with both hands and spun around it twice before letting go. She landed beside the purse-snatcher and the victim three seconds before Robin touched down.

Robin cracked his knuckles. "You win," he told Batgirl. "I guess you get the first crack at him."

The woman and purse-snatcher both raised their hands.

"Wait," the woman said. "We were just acting."

"What?" asked Batgirl. "Are you in a play or something?"

"No," the purse-snatcher replied, shaking his head. "This really weird guy paid us to just pretend."

The woman nodded her head. Then she reached into her purse and pulled out a green envelope.

"And he said if you two showed up, we were supposed to give you this," the woman explained.

Batgirl took the envelope. Robin moved in as they both examined it closely. It read, "To: Robin & Batgirl, From: ?"

"Let me guess. Skinny guy? Dressed in green? Has a thing for question marks?" Robin asked. But the man and woman were already gone.

Batgirl opened the envelope. She pulled out a green card and read what was written on it. "I squawk, hiss, snort, and growl. I giggle, chirp, roar, and howl. What am I?"

Robin slowly shook his head. "Another riddle from the Riddler."

"What kind of animal makes *all* those sounds?" Batgirl asked.

"Maybe he means a group of animals," Robin suggested. "Like on a nature program."

Batgirl's lips tightened. "Except for the giggle part." Then she snapped her fingers. "The answer is a zoo. The kids who visit are the ones who giggle."

"Excellent," Robin said as he reached into his Utility Belt. He pulled out his phone and searched the internet.

"Gotham City Zoo just received a priceless baby panda today," he announced.

"And the Riddler's going to steal it," Batgirl finished.

"Not if I can help it," Robin said. He put his phone away and pulled out his grapnel. He aimed it at the nearest building.

"Wait, Robin." Batgirl caught his arm. "What about what Batman said? We're not supposed to go up against the heavy hitters alone. Doesn't the Riddler count as a heavy hitter?"

Robin sighed. "One: The Riddler isn't so tough. And two: We're not going alone. We have each other."

Batgirl frowned. "I'm not sure that's what Batman meant."

"Sure it is," Robin said as he fired his grapnel. "Come on."

* * *

WHOOSH! WHOOSH!

Robin and Batgirl swung from buildings and ran across rooftops until they reached the Gotham City Zoo. They vaulted over the closed front gate and marched down the main walkway. Small streetlights lit the wide path before them.

"The zoo looks quiet to me," Batgirl said, scanning the nearby exhibits. "Do you think we got the riddle wrong?"

Robin stopped in his tracks and held up a finger. "Wait. You hear that?"

RUUUUMMMMBLE!

Batgirl cocked her head as a deep, low rumble grew louder and louder. The sound soon became almost deafening. Then an unusual stampede ran out from the shadows.

"Look out!" Batgirl warned as she leaped into the air. Robin did the same as they both were almost trampled by runaway elephants, rhinos, and hippos.

The young crime fighters jumped from the back of one beast to another as the humongous herd galloped beneath them. Robin and Batgirl finally somersaulted to the ground as the huge beasts ran on.

"That was close!" Robin exclaimed.

"No kidding," Batgirl agreed. "But now we know we solved the riddle correctly. The Riddler is here, all right."

"That was probably supposed to be a diversion." Robin glanced around. "I'll find Nygma. You go after the baby panda."

"Good idea," Batgirl said. She took off in one direction, and the Boy Wonder darted in the other.

* * *

Batgirl followed the brand-new signs directing the public toward the panda enclosure. She turned a corner and spotted a large box truck parked beside the panda exhibit. A black-and-white object sat in the cage deep in the back of the truck.

Batgirl leaped onto the truck and crept toward the cage.

"Don't worry, little guy," Batgirl said as she moved closer to the cage. "I'll get you out of there."

The young hero pulled out her lock-pick set, preparing to open the cage door. Then she noticed something odd about the baby panda. It wasn't a panda at all. It was just a stuffed panda toy.

"Wait a minute," Batgirl said just before a set of bars fell down behind her.

KLANK!

She found herself trapped in a larger cage inside the truck.

* * *

Meanwhile, Robin couldn't find the Riddler anywhere. He was about to circle back toward Batgirl when something smacked against the side of his head.

WHACK!

"Hey!" Robin shouted.

The hero ducked as another object flew past him. It was an apple. A banana shot in from another direction. Soon, he was pelted by fruit from all directions.

The Boy Wonder sprang toward the trees to get away from the attack. He landed on a thick branch and found himself surrounded by his attackers.

The tree limbs were full of all kinds of monkeys. Their arms were loaded with fruit as they continued to hurl them his way.

"I'm not fighting monkeys," Robin said as he swung from tree to tree. In their natural element, the hairy attackers easily gave chase. They never let up, pelting him with fruit all the way.

Robin was so busy trying to get away that he didn't see the rope net until it was too late.

SNATCH!

As soon as Robin slammed into it, the net tightened around him. The trap was controlled by a thin rope leading up to a branch and then down to the Riddler himself.

"And Robin makes two," the villain said as he pulled the net tighter. The young crime fighter was bound so tightly he couldn't break free. "This is what a *real* zoo crew can do!" the Riddler said as he burst into laughter.

CHAPTER 3

ROOFTOP RIDDLE

Batman spread his cape and glided down to the dark rooftop. He tucked and rolled into a somersault. He sprang to his feet and glanced around, making sure he was alone.

The Dark Knight tapped his mask just behind his right ear. "Robin, Batgirl, come in," he said. For the fourth time, there was still no reply.

"This isn't like them," he said to himself. "Something must be wrong."

Suddenly, a bright light appeared across the city. A large spotlight shone onto the clouds above. It was the Bat-Signal!

Batman pulled out his grapnel and prepared to leap off the rooftop. He skidded to a stop before he reached the edge.

"That's not the Bat-Signal," he growled.

Normally, the spotlight had a symbol of a bat in the center. This signal had a large question mark instead.

"Edward Nygma." Batman tightened his lips as he dove from the rooftop. He shot his grapnel, and its hook flew toward a nearby skyscraper. It latched onto the building, and Batman used the attached Batrope to swing toward the next rooftop. Soon he landed atop the police station, next to a large spotlight.

Batman was about to switch off the light when he noticed a small green box on the roof. As he stepped closer, the box's lid blew off with a shower of sparks and confetti.

POOF!

Batman shielded himself with his cape, but it turned out to be a harmless explosion. When the sparks had died away, a life-size, 3-D hologram of the Riddler appeared.

"Hello, Batman," the image said.

"What do you want, Nygma?" asked the crime fighter.

"Oh, I won't answer, Batman. This is just a recording," the Riddler's image said. "But I think it's one you'll find most rewarding."

Batman crossed his arms. It sounded as if he was in for another one of Nygma's riddles.

"Now, give this puzzle a whirl," the image continued. "If you wish to save Batgirl."

Batman stiffened. So she and Robin were in trouble.

The image of the Riddler twirled his cane. "Her fate will be decided if or whether you're clever enough to piece this together." He tipped his hat. "No more taunts. No more teases. Soon she may just fall to pieces."

Batman didn't like the sound of that at all.

The Riddler's recording continued. "Now Robin's riddle is a little half-baked. A few clever words . . . give or take." The Riddler shrugged. "The boy's fortune will simply be undone, if you don't find him before the morning sun."

The Riddler spread his arms wide. "Solve these riddles or I can save you the trouble. Just get to 433 Thunderbrook on the double." He gave a sly grin. "If you want them safe, you have but to ask. As long as you first take off your mask."

The image of the Riddler disappeared, and the rooftop was dark once again.

"It sounds as if Robin and Batgirl didn't listen to my warning," Batman said. "They took on the Riddler without any backup." He shook his head. "And the Riddler will only let them go if I reveal my secret identity."

Batman ran toward the edge of the roof. "I think I may need some backup of my own." He spread his cape wide and dove into the night.

* * *

The Riddler paced back and forth atop the large shipping container. He glanced around the abandoned warehouse and checked his watch.

"The time has come," the Riddler said to himself. "The stage is set."

The full moon shone through the windows above, creating large shafts of light. The Riddler's twenty henchmen milled in and out of the light as they all waited for the main attraction—the unmasking of Batman.

Suddenly, the warehouse door rolled open and a familiar shape appeared in the doorway.

"Welcome, welcome my old friend," the Riddler said. "You arrived in the nick of time." He held up his cane, pointing out a red button on the handle. "Any longer and I would've pushed this button, sending your little bat friends to their terrible fate."

The Dark Knight didn't reply. He slowly marched through the empty warehouse, moving in and out of the shafts of light. The surrounding henchmen picked up pipes and chains and prepared for a fight.

The Riddler raised his cane, thumb hovering over the button. "That is far enough, Batman."

The Dark Knight froze. His black silhouette was completely motionless.

"I used to think the ultimate riddle was how to defeat you," the Riddler said. "But I did that when I captured your puny sidekicks." A wide grin stretched across his face.

"Now I think the ultimate riddle is: Who is Batman?" The Riddler pointed down at the Dark Knight. "So take off your mask!"

At first, Batman didn't move. Then he reached up and pulled back his mask.

The henchmen held their breath with anticipation. The Riddler let out a small chuckle.

Batman let his mask and cape fall to the ground. However, he was still in the shadows, so only the dark outline of a man could be seen.

"Now, step into the light," Riddler ordered.

There was another pause before the dark figure stepped forward. He moved into a shaft of light and his identity was revealed.

The Riddler gasped. "Nightwing?!!"

Nightwing grinned and took a fighting stance. He reached up and pulled his fighting batons from his back.

"I couldn't let Batman have all the fun," Nightwing said.

The Riddler snarled and pressed the button on his cane.

THE SIDEKICK SAVE

Batgirl almost had her ropes untied. She was trapped inside an old printing building. And from the looks of all the puzzle pieces scattered about, the company had once created jigsaw puzzles.

Batgirl had heard on the news that the old building was going to be demolished soon. She just didn't think she'd be inside it when it happened. Light from the full moon shone through the broken skylight above. The moonlight revealed the dozens of explosive packs attached to the columns around her.

Like the many bombs, Batgirl was attached to one of the columns. But not for long. She pulled at one of the knots with her teeth, trying to free herself.

BEEP! BEEP! BEEP! BEEP!

Suddenly, the explosive packs beeped all around her. Numbers appeared on the screens of every one. Their timers turned on and began counting down from thirty.

"I only have thirty seconds before these go off," Batgirl said to herself. She struggled harder at loosening the ropes. She had just enough time to free herself, but not enough time to get out of the building. "I'm not going to make it."

WHOOSH!

The room darkened as something swooped overhead, blocking out the moonlight.

Batgirl looked up to see a giant Bat-Signal in the sky. Except that it wasn't really the Bat-Signal. It was the Batplane, hovering in front of the moon.

A hatch opened at the bottom of the plane, and Batman appeared. He dropped down on a long, thin cable. He lowered through the skylight and toward Batgirl.

The young crime fighter slipped out of the last rope just as Batman came within reach. She glanced at one of the timers. "Ten seconds before this place blows."

"Grab on," Batman ordered as he reached down to her.

Batgirl leaped up and grabbed his arm. Batman pressed a remote and the jet began to rise. When they were halfway to the skylight, the explosives went off.

KA·FOOOOOOM!!!

The building crumbled around them as they rose higher and higher. The Batplane finally hoisted them up and away from the destruction below. The cable retracted, pulling them back through the open hatch. Once they were safe aboard the jet, it sped into the night.

"How did you find me?" Batgirl asked.

"One of Nygma's riddles," Batman replied. "He called it a puzzle and said you may fall to pieces. I knew this puzzle factory was due for demolition."

"What about Robin?" Batgirl asked.

"I haven't figured that riddle out yet," Batman admitted. "The boy's fortune will be undone, if you don't find him before the morning sun."

"I think I know the answer," Batgirl said. "I've seen fortune cookies from a place called Morning Sun Bakery."

"Hmmm, Nygma did say that his riddle was half-baked. That must be where he's holding Robin." Batman steered the plane toward East Gotham. "Good work, Batgirl."

"Thanks," she said. "And sorry about going against the Riddler alone."

"We'll talk about that later," Batman replied. "Let's find Robin, fast."

* * *

Robin couldn't tell where he was, but it smelled delicious. His nostrils were filled with the scents of freshly baked bread and pastries. Unfortunately, he couldn't really enjoy anything because his hands and feet were tied tightly.

Robin also noticed he was at the bottom of some kind of large bowl. Since he was in such a cramped space, he had a tough time escaping his bindings. The ropes were knotted behind him. It was all he could do to loosen a single knot.

Suddenly, Robin jolted forward. He could see the ceiling move above him as his bowl glided down some sort of track.

"This can't be good," Robin grumbled to himself.

Then the bowl tipped sideways and Robin rolled out. He could finally see where he was. He was on a long conveyor belt in an automated bakery. Several balls of dough rode the belt ahead of him and behind him.

"I was right," Robin said. "This isn't good at all."

Down the line, the balls of dough moved between two long rolling pins. Once they were flattened, a large press dropped and cut the dough into shapes. Other machines inserted paper fortunes and folded the dough before everything headed into a large oven.

"At least I don't have to worry about the oven," Robin said. "I won't make it past the rollers and cutters."

Just before he reached the rolling pins, Robin rolled onto his feet and hopped down the conveyor belt. "I got this," he said. "I got this."

But then his feet hit a ball of dough, and he fell backward. He was about to get up again when his cape became caught between the rolling pins.

"Then again," Robin said as he planted his feet on the belt, "maybe I don't."

The Boy Wonder pushed with all of his might as the rollers pulled him closer and closer.

WHIP-PANG!

A Batarang whistled through the air and stuck between the rollers. The machine smoked as it strained against the weapon blocking it. Finally, it shut down completely.

"Ah, I almost had it," Robin said as Batman and Batgirl ran up to the smoking conveyor belt.

"Yeah, I could see that," Batgirl said as she untied the Boy Wonder.

Batman pried open the rollers and pulled Robin's cape free.

Robin rubbed the back of his head and looked at the Dark Knight. "I have a feeling that there's a lecture coming."

"That depends," said Batman. "Do you need one?"

Robin sighed. "Not really. We get it. Don't go after the heavy hitters alone."

"*Alone*, meaning without Batman," Batgirl added.

Batman nodded. "Right."

"I definitely learned my lesson," Robin said. "And I don't think I'll be able to eat a fortune cookie ever again."

CHAPTER 5

ONE FINAL RIDDLE

Nightwing leaned way back as one of the Riddler's henchmen swung a heavy chain at him. The steel links passed harmlessly overhead as the crime fighter back-flipped and landed on his feet. Without stopping, Nightwing used his batons to block attacks from two other pipe-wielding criminals.

Nightwing grinned up at the Riddler. "Funny, I remember your henchmen being tougher."

Still standing atop the large shipping container, the Riddler snarled and pointed down at the young crime fighter. "Get him!"

Four more henchmen rushed Nightwing at once. He jumped up, kicked off the chest of one of the men, and leaped toward another. He grabbed one crook's arm in midair and flipped him over his shoulder. The criminal flew into the remaining two henchmen.

SKREEEEE!

The sound of squealing tires echoed throughout the warehouse. Nightwing braced himself as a forklift drove out of the shadows. It raised its two sharp tines and aimed them at the crime fighter. It sped closer.

Nightwing easily dodged the approaching machine, and it whipped past him. But then two more forklifts raced toward him.

Nightwing got clear of one forklift but not the other. The machine's fork caught him under his arms and lifted him off his feet.

Before Nightwing could escape, the henchman drove the forklift toward the huge shipping container. The forklift crashed into the container, stabbing its fork deep into the thin steel. Nightwing was pinned between the forklift and the side of the container.

"You should've listened to Batman," the Riddler taunted from above. "Don't go up against the heavy hitters alone."

Nightwing couldn't escape. The forklift pushed forward, squeezing him between the machine and the steel container. However, the young hero simply laughed.

"Okay, a lot to unpack there," Nightwing said. "First of all, don't flatter yourself. You're not what I'd call a heavy hitter."

The Riddler snarled in reply.

"Second, as you can see, I'm not a kid anymore," Nightwing continued. "I don't have that rule."

"Well, maybe you should," the Riddler said with a laugh. "You didn't do too well coming here alone."

Nightwing raised a finger. "Ah! You see, that's my third point . . . I'm not really alone." The crime fighter looked up into the rafters.

The Riddler followed his gaze and saw Batman, Robin, and Batgirl perched on a long ceiling beam.

"A little help here," Nightwing said.

Batman's hand was a blur as it sent a Batarang flying toward the forklift.

SWISH!

The weapon struck the control lever, causing the machine to back up. The fork pulled out of the steel container and Nightwing was free. The crime fighter jumped clear of the forklift before the driver could trap him again.

Batman, Robin, and Batgirl split up as they dove from the warehouse ceiling. They each took on a group of henchmen, while Nightwing went after the forklift driver. He leaped for the forklift and grabbed the top of its cage. He swung around in a wide circle, kicking the driver out of his seat.

As Batgirl rocketed down, she smashed into one of the henchmen. Riding him like a human skateboard, she jumped off his back and sent him tumbling across the floor. He slammed into two more henchmen, knocking them down like bowling pins.

Robin landed in the middle of three crooks. He ducked and dodged as all of them swung long pipes at him. The criminals were so focused on the Boy Wonder, they didn't pay attention as he easily dodged their attacks. The henchmen ended up hitting each other instead.

Batman touched down on the warehouse floor and remained motionless. Then, as four crooks charged him, he threw down a single smoke pellet. The henchmen ran into a cloud of smoke where the Dark Knight had been standing. A few grunts, shouts, and yells later, the smoke cleared and all the crooks were tied in a bundle on the floor.

"Enough!" shouted the Riddler.

The four heroes stood together, surrounded by the remaining henchmen. They paused their battle at the sound of Riddler's voice.

"I had a feeling you would try something like this," Nygma explained. "So I have one final riddle: What's black and has eight hairy legs?"

"Let me guess," Robin said, crossing his arms. "A spider?"

"Nope." The Riddler shook his head and grinned. "Not even close."

The villain tapped his cane on the roof of the shipping container. Two henchmen ran to the end of the container and swung its doors open. The ground shook as four giant gorillas charged out. They each wore green vests and hats like the Riddler's.

"Or . . . four gorillas." Robin shrugged. "That was my second guess."

Nightwing raised an eyebrow. "Wow. You don't see that every day."

Batgirl rubbed the back of her neck and glanced up at Batman. "Uh, did we mention that the Riddler caught us in a zoo?"

"Capture the gorillas," Batman ordered. "But don't hurt them."

"Easier said than done," Nightwing said as he dodged the first gorilla attack. He somersaulted over the beast's massive fists.

Batman threw his bolas at one of the apes. The heavy balls at the end of the ropes encircled the animal, wrapping it tightly. The gorilla roared and flexed its arms, snapping the ropes as if they were thread.

"Maybe this will work," Batgirl said as she leaped high into the air, away from two grabbing gorillas. She flipped backward, her arms spread wide. She opened her hands to release two nets. The webbing expanded and ensnared each of the gorillas.

The beasts growled and snarled as they struggled against their bonds. Then, one by one, they broke free.

"They're too strong," Nightwing said. "We have to think of something else."

Robin shook his head. "This is all my fault," he said as he ran for the nearest gorilla. "I'll take care of it."

"No, Robin," Batman scolded.

Robin didn't listen. Instead, he hopped onto one gorilla's back and grabbed his oversized hat. He pulled it down over the ape's eyes.

Robin leaped to the next gorilla and did the same to his hat. Then he grabbed the third gorilla's vest collar and pulled it down over the beast's shoulders. The Boy Wonder then did the hat trick on the fourth gorilla.

"What is he doing?" asked Batgirl.

Nightwing shrugged. "Really annoying them?"

The four apes roared with rage as they tried to untangle themselves from their clothes. When they were finally free, they only had eyes for Robin. They ignored the other heroes as they chased the young crime fighter back toward the shipping container. He ran through the open doors, and the gorillas followed.

"Think he can pull this off?" Nightwing asked as he and Batgirl ran toward the container.

"He'd better," Batgirl said. "Or he's going to be a gorilla punching bag in there."

"Now!" Robin shouted as he dove out of the shipping container.

Batgirl and Nightwing slammed the doors and threw the latches just as the gorillas reached them. The entire container rocked back and forth as the apes crashed into the locked doors.

Meanwhile, the Riddler huffed as he sprinted across the top of the container. He glanced over his shoulder to make sure none of the crime fighters were following him as he escaped. That's when he ran into a brick wall. Actually, it only *felt* like a brick wall. Nygma fell to the ground after smashing into Batman himself.

The Riddler scrambled to his feet and swung his cane at the Dark Knight. Batman caught it under one arm and wrenched it from the criminal's grasp. He snapped it over his knee like a twig.

Nygma stumbled back and fell down again. He raised his hands. "I surrender! I surrender!"

"Now where have I heard that before?" Batman said with a smirk. He cuffed the criminal's outstretched hands.

Batgirl appeared and added her own pair of cuffs to the crook's wrists. "He's not escaping this time."

Robin added his own cuffs and smiled up at Batman. "And we did it together."

The Riddler looked up at them with half a smile. "At least that means I'm a heavy hitter, right?"

"Eh, not really," Nightwing said with a shrug. "And you'll have plenty of time to figure out why in prison."

The Riddler

REAL NAME: Edward Nygma

OCCUPATION: Professional Criminal

BASE: Gotham City

HEIGHT: 6 feet, 1 inch

WEIGHT: 183 lbs.

EYES: Blue

HAIR: Black

POWERS/ABILITIES: Genius level intelligence, a vast knowledge of subjects, and a keen knack for creating puzzles and riddles. He is also skilled with technology, allowing him to invent things to carry out his devious plans.

BIOGRAPHY:

Even as a little boy, Edward Nygma loved riddles and puzzles. When he grew up, Nygma turned his passion into a career. He became a video game designer and soon invented a popular game called *Riddle of the Minotaur*. The game sold millions of copies, but Nygma didn't receive a dime from the manufacturer. To get his revenge, Nygma became the Riddler, a cryptic criminal who leaves clues to his crimes.

- The Riddler's cane is shaped like a question mark. This weapon can deliver a shocking blast—the Riddler's answer to his toughest problems.

- The Riddler doesn't just want to break the law. He wants to outsmart Batman as well. Before every crime, the Riddler first sends a clue to Batman.

- The Riddler's real name suits him perfectly. Edward Nygma, or E. Nygma for short, sounds like the word "enigma," which means a mysterious person.

- Harry Houdini is one of the Riddler's greatest heroes. This real-life magician is famous for his stunts, tricks, and great escapes.

BIOGRAPHIES

Author

Michael Anthony Steele has been in the entertainment industry for more than twenty-five years writing for television, movies, and video games. He has authored more than 110 books for exciting characters and brands including Batman, Superman, Green Lantern, Spider-Man, Shrek, Scooby-Doo, LEGO City, Garfield, Winx Club, Night at the Museum, and The Penguins of Madagascar. Mr. Steele lives on a ranch in Texas, but he enjoys meeting his readers when he visits schools and libraries all over the country.

Illustrator

Leonel Castellani has worked as a comic artist and illustrator for more than twenty years. Mostly known for his work on licensed art for companies such as Warner Bros., DC Comics, Disney, Marvel Entertainment, and Cartoon Network, Leonel has also built a career as a conceptual designer and storyboard artist for video games, movies, and TV. In addition to drawing, Leonel also likes to sculpt and paint. He currently lives in La Plata City, Argentina.

GLOSSARY

automated (aw-tah-MAY-ted)—a mechanical process programmed to follow a set of instructions by itself

baton (buh-TAHN)—a small bat or rod used to block punches and knock back attacks

conveyor belt (kuhn-VAY-uhr BELT)—a moving belt that carries objects from one place to another

demolition (de-muh-LI-shuhn)—blowing up or taking down a structure on purpose

district (DIS-trikt)—a zone, area, or region in a city

fate (FAYT)—events in a person's life that are out of that person's control or are said to be determined by a supernatural power

grapnel (GRAP-nuhl)—a grappling hook connected to a rope that can be fired like a gun

silhouette (sil-oo-ET)—an outline of something that shows its shape

stampede (stam-PEED)—when a group of animals makes a sudden, wild rush in one direction, usually because something has frightened them

unconscious (uhn-KON-shuhss)—not awake; not able to see, feel, or think

DISCUSSION QUESTIONS

1. Batman's rule is that Robin and Batgirl can't take on any major villains on their own. Do you think they break that rule when they go after the Riddler? Provide reasons to explain your answer.

2. The Riddler believes the ultimate riddle is the truth behind Batman's secret identity. Why does the Prince of Puzzles want to know the Dark Knight's true identity? How might that information help the villain in the future?

3. Teamwork plays a big part in this story. Think of three times where the heroes had to work together to solve a problem or defeat an enemy. Discuss how working together, rather than alone, helped them succeed.

WRITING PROMPTS

1. In this story, Batman must save Robin and Batgirl from the Riddler. But imagine that the tables are turned. Write a short story where the Riddler captures the Dark Knight instead. Describe how Batman's sidekicks save him from the villain.

2. The Riddler creates riddles that Batman must solve to find the locations of Batgirl and Robin. Think of a well-known place in your own community—such as the library or grocery store. Write a riddle that gives clues about the place without naming it. Then give the riddle to your friends and see if they can guess the location.

3. The Riddler surprises the heroes by releasing four gorillas from the shipping container. But what if the container didn't hold gorillas? Think of something else—such as mutant spiders or robots—that could have been hiding in it. Write a new scene describing how the heroes defeat the new enemies.